Pearl vs. the Tooth Fairy

by Natasha Wing

Illustrated by Lynne Avril

Scholastic Inc.

New York   Toronto   London   Auckland   Sydney
Mexico City   New Delhi   Hong Kong   Buenos Aires

To Debbie Hartman and Barrie Love,
for opening windows to other worlds
—N. W.

To Ellie
— Grandmalynnie

ISBN-13: 978-0-545-08577-9
ISBN-10: 0-545-08577-2

Text copyright © 2009 by Natasha Wing
Illustrations copyright © 2009 by Scholastic Inc.

12 11 10 9 8 7 6 5 4 3 2 1   9 10 11 12 13 14/0

Printed in the U.S.A.
First printing, January 2009

Book design by Jennifer Rinaldi Windau

Contents

1. The Lost Lost Tooth

Pearl Ruby was a collector.

Pearl collected banana stickers. She collected rocks shaped like hearts. She collected curly ribbons.

She always saved clippings of her hair. She put them in an envelope. Then she filed them in her "Hair" box.

"Honestly, Pearl," said her mother, "is there room for one more envelope?"

Pearl didn't hear her.

She was planning her next collection.

Pearl took out her book on the human body. She opened to a page with a drawing of a mouth. The drawing showed all the teeth. They had funny names.

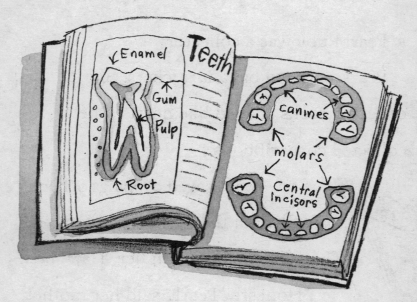

Her bottom front tooth was called a central incisor. That was the tooth that was ready to fall out!

Pearl's first tooth was loose. She had tried lots of ways to make it fall out.

She jiggled it.

She swished water in her mouth.

She poked it with a straw.

"That tooth is stuck on like glue," said Dad.

But not anymore. She flicked it with her tongue. It stuck straight out. Yet it still held on.

Pearl wanted to put her tooth in a special box. She checked her closet.

A shoe box? Too big.

A paperclip box? Too small.

Then she remembered she had a pretty jewelry box. Mom had given it to her. It was gold with a little lock. The inside was lined with blue velvet.

"Perfect."

Pearl got out her beads. She glued silver ones on the box. She placed them in the shape of a smile. She labeled the box "Teeth."

Mom poked her head in. "Brush your teeth before bed."

Pearl brushed her teeth. She was careful. She didn't want to spit her loose tooth down the drain.

But her big sister, Opal, was in the way.

"Gross!" said Opal. She wiped Pearl's spit off her arm.

"Don't forget to floss!" Mom called. "Especially you, Pearl."

Pearl pulled out a long string of floss. *Zip!* She slid it between her teeth.

"Hey!" said Opal. "You got the last piece!"

Opal grabbed the string and pulled.

"Ouch!" shouted Pearl.

Pearl heard a clink in the sink.

"Don't blame me!" Opal ran from the bathroom.

"What's going on?" asked Dad.

"My tooth!" cried Pearl. She pointed to the drain. "It's gone!"

2. Dear Tooth Fairy

"Super plumber to the rescue!" shouted Dad.

Dad got his toolbox. He scooted under the sink. He pulled out a pipe bent like a U.

"Towel."

Pearl put a towel out on the floor. Dad turned the pipe upside down.

An earring fell out. *Plink.*

Then a tiny screw fell out. *Plunk.*

Finally, Pearl's tooth fell out.

Pearl picked it up.

"Look at those ridges," she said. "This tooth

can cut through beef jerky."

"That tooth bit my finger when you were a baby," said Dad. He honked her nose.

Pearl laughed. She had a gap in her smile now.

Mom came into the bathroom. "What's all the fuss?"

Pearl held up her tooth.

"Wow!" said Mom. "You lost your first tooth."

Pearl beamed.

"You know what that means," said Dad. He winked at Mom.

"Tell me!" said Pearl.

"The Tooth Fairy is coming for your tooth tonight."

Pearl ran to her room.

She placed her tooth in her gold box. She locked it shut.

Mom came to tuck her in. "The Tooth Fairy will be here soon."

"She isn't going to find anything," said Pearl.

Mom lifted the pillow. "Where's your tooth?"

Pearl zipped her lips.

Mom looked around the room. There were hundreds of secret hiding places.

"How will the Tooth Fairy find your tooth if you hide it?" Mom asked.

Pearl shrugged.

Mom said, "Then you won't get any money."

"That's okay. I want to keep my tooth."

"All righty. You better write her a note."

She handed Pearl a pen and paper. Then she kissed her good night.

Later that night, the Tooth Fairy flew in through Pearl's window. She tiptoed onto

Pearl's bed. She checked under the pillow.

"What's this?" She read Pearl's letter.

"Oh, great. A troublemaker."

3. All That Glitters

Pearl woke up early. She reached under her pillow and found a note. It was written on glitter paper.

Dear Pearl,
I was surprised when I stopped by your bed last night. You didn't leave your tooth! I collect teeth, too. That's my job. I take them back to Fairyland, I live in a castle made of teeth. Love.
Tooth Fairy

"She's a collector, too!" said Pearl.

Then she read the P.S.

P.S. Leave your tooth under your pillow. I'll come back tonight. Your tooth is VERY important to me.

Pearl reached for her gold box. It was hidden between her penny collection and her gum-wrapper collection.

Her tooth was still in the box.

The Tooth Fairy has billions of teeth. Why is this one so important? Pearl thought.

Pearl brought the letter to breakfast.

"Look what I got from the Tooth Fairy," she said.

Dad looked at Mom.

Mom said, "When did you put your tooth under your pillow?"

"I didn't," said Pearl.

Mom and Dad frowned.

They read the glitter letter.

"Isn't that sweet, Tom," said Mom. "She brings the teeth to Fairyland."

Dad sipped his coffee.

Opal giggled.

Pearl pointed to the P.S.

"I don't get this part. Why is my tooth *very* important to her?"

"For the same reason it's important to you,"
said Mom. "The Tooth Fairy is a collector."

Pearl got a straw. She sipped milk through
the gap in her teeth.

"Why does she have to come back?" asked
Pearl. "I told her I'm keeping my tooth."

"Maybe she thinks you'll change your mind," said Mom.

"That will never happen," said Opal. She rolled her eyes.

Pearl put her hands on her hips. "I don't want money."

Mom asked, "What would you like instead? Stickers? Cat socks?"

"I already have what I want," said Pearl. "My tooth."

4. Fairy Money

Pearl saved a seat on the school bus. It was for her best friend, Lanie.

Lanie got on the bus at the next stop.

"Showsies," said Lanie.

Pearl showed Lanie the new gap in her teeth.

"It fell out last night," said Pearl.

"So did mine!" said Lanie.

Lanie did showsies. She had two holes. One was on the bottom. And a new one was on the top.

Lanie reached in her pocket. She pulled out a glitter dollar.

"It's a Tooth Fairy dollar," said Lanie. "It matches my nail polish." She held out her hand.

"Let's see your glitter dollar," said Lanie.

"I didn't get one," said Pearl.

Andrew popped up behind them. "Ha-ha!" he said. "The Tooth Fairy forgot you."

"No, she didn't," said Pearl.

She opened her letter from the Tooth Fairy.

"It glitters!" said Lanie.

Lanie read the letter. Her mouth dropped open. "I *knew* she lived in a castle."

Andrew yelled, "That's fake!"

He pointed at Pearl. "*You* wrote it. *You* put glitter on it."

"Did not."

Andrew bounced up and down. "Fake, fake, fake."

"Sit down, Andrew!" yelled the bus driver.

Lanie scratched her head. "Why didn't you give the Tooth Fairy your tooth?"

"What if I knock out a tooth?" said Pearl. "I'd have a spare."

Pearl saw a guy on TV get a glass eye. He kept his real eyeball in a jar.

"You can't keep your tooth, Pearl," said Lanie. "You have to give it to the Tooth Fairy."

"Says who?"

"Says everyone on the planet," said Lanie.

Pearl laughed. Lanie said everyone on the planet liked milk chocolate, too.

She was wrong. Pearl liked white chocolate better.

"I'm starting a collection," said Pearl.

"Dodo brain," Andrew said. "You can't keep your tooth."

"Why not?" Pearl asked.

"Because it belongs to the Tooth Fairy. You have to give it to her. Or else she'll turn you into a toad." Andrew smirked.

Pearl said, "She won't miss one tooth."

Lanie bit her nail. "But she's coming back for it. What are you going to do?"

Pearl had to think fast. She didn't want to be turned into a toad.

5. Trader

Lanie opened her lunch box.

"Yuck!" she said.

Her mom had packed a ham sandwich. She had packed trail mix. She had also packed three rubbery carrots.

"It must be food shopping day," said Lanie.

She picked through the trail mix. She ate the nuts and the dried fruit. But not the white chocolate chips.

"Can I have them?" Pearl asked.

"I'll trade you for your dippers."

"Okay."

That gave Pearl an idea. *Collectors don't just save stuff. They trade stuff, too!*

Pearl thought hard all through math. *What can I trade my tooth for?*

She looked through her desk. She found a pen.

Yes! The Tooth Fairy writes notes!

But how big is the Tooth Fairy? This pen might be too big for her to hold.

An eraser? No. She has a magic wand to fix mistakes.

Pearl got off the bus after school. She went to the lot next door. A new house was being built there.

It was Friday. The workers had left early.

Pearl always found treasures in the lot. Last time she found colored wire.

Maybe there was something the Tooth Fairy might want.

Pearl found a roll of tape.

She put it down. What would the Tooth Fairy do with tape?

She found a screwdriver. Maybe she could use it to open a window.

She put that down, too. *Duh. Fairies use magic to open windows.*

Pearl found two feathers on a pile of dirt. Aha!

Pearl's mom was waiting by the front door of their house. She had a camera.

"Smile!" said Mom.

Pearl smiled a pumpkin grin. *Click!*

Mom printed the photo. She put it in a frame.

The new photo sat next to an old photo of Pearl.

"Look," said Mom. "There you are with your first baby tooth. And here you are with your first lost tooth."

Pearl set the frame on her bedside table.

The photo was nice. But it wasn't as good as keeping her tooth.

Mom tucked Pearl in that night.

She lifted Pearl's pillow.

No tooth.

"I guess you didn't change your mind."

"Nope," said Pearl.

Dear Tooth Fairy,
    I'm trading you these feathers for my tooth. Maybe they can help you fly faster. I hope you like them!
    ☺ Pearl

The Tooth Fairy landed with a crash in Pearl's room. She bent her wand. She ripped her dress.

"Pesky window screen!"

She was not happy with what Pearl had left her.

"I'm getting sick of this."

She scribbled another letter. She signed her name. Then she dotted the "i" so hard she poked a hole in the paper.

6. Fair-y Trade

The feathers were still on Pearl's table the next morning. There was a note, too.

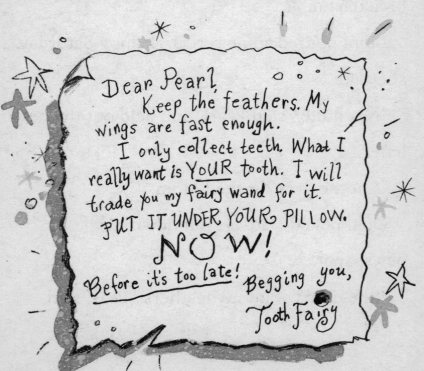

Dear Pearl,
Keep the feathers. My wings are fast enough.
I only collect teeth. What I really want is YOUR tooth. I will trade you my fairy wand for it.
PUT IT UNDER YOUR PILLOW.
NOW!
Before it's too late! Begging you,
Tooth Fairy

Pearl was glad she didn't get turned into a toad.

Maybe she *should* trade the Tooth Fairy for her wand. She could turn Andrew into a toad! Opal, too.

But what if she didn't want to trade?

Pearl thumped downstairs. She sat at the breakfast table.

Mom poured some cereal. "Happy Saturday," she said.

"Not quite," said Pearl. She held out the new letter.

"Another one?" asked Mom.

Opal poked Dad. He put down his newspaper.

"She didn't want my feathers," Pearl said.

"Stubborn," said Dad. "Like someone else I know."

Mom frowned. "What does she want this time?"

"The same thing. My tooth," said Pearl.

Mom read the letter out loud. "She sounds a bit . . . mad."

"Super mad," added Opal.

"Maybe she's in a bad mood," said Pearl. "She didn't sign the letter 'love' this time."

Mom brushed the hair out of Pearl's face. "Are you in a bad mood, sweetie?"

Pearl pushed her cereal around with her spoon. She hadn't taken one bite.

"Are you having trouble with someone?" asked Mom.

Pearl shrugged.

"It's best to talk it out. Face to face," Mom added.

Pearl had never seen the Tooth Fairy. How was she going to talk face to face?

7. Bad Mood

Soccer practice was bad. Pearl let shot after shot go by.

Lanie pumped her fists. "Come on, Pearl! You can do it!"

An easy shot came at the goal. Pearl's shoes felt as heavy as stone. She missed the ball.

Pearl felt like the worst goalie ever.

Coach gave her a pep talk. "You are our top goalie. I know you'll play better at the game tomorrow."

Coach high-fived Pearl.

Lanie tried to cheer Pearl up after practice. She showed off her new mood ring. She got the ring with her tooth money.

"Try it on!" said Lanie.

"No, thanks," said Pearl. She didn't need a ring to tell her what kind of mood she was in.

"Did your trade work?" asked Lanie.

"No. The Tooth Fairy doesn't want my feathers. She wants to trade her wand for my tooth."

"OH MY GOSH!" cried Lanie.

"*Shhhh*," cried Pearl.

"Do you know what you can do with a fairy wand?" said Lanie.

Zap myself into a good mood, thought Pearl.

"You could make ice cream!" said Lanie. She waved a pretend wand. *Poof!*

She aimed her pretend wand at the soccer field. "You could make our team win!"

Pearl groaned.

"Think about it," said Lanie. "You'll be the only person ON THE PLANET with a real fairy wand."

Pearl thought of another good reason to trade her tooth for the wand.

Then the Tooth Fairy would quit bugging her.

8. Big Mess

It was bedtime. Pearl's mom brought her a mug of warm milk. It had whipped cream and white chocolate shavings on top. It was Pearl's favorite.

"Drink it. You'll sleep better." Mom kissed Pearl on the head. "See you in the morning."

Pearl drank her warm milk. She read the Tooth Fairy's letter again.

Why would she give away her one-and-only magic wand?

Then the words "Before it's too late" jumped

out at her. Too late for what?

Mom did say it was best to talk things out. Face to face.

That's it! She would talk to the Tooth Fairy. She'd tell her she wouldn't trade her tooth. Not for a fairy wand. Not for anything.

She held her eyes open until she couldn't . . .

stay awake . . .

any . . .

longer.

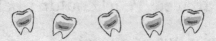

The Tooth Fairy landed in a huff. She had bags under her eyes.

She had never had such trouble getting a tooth before!

"This kid is the worst. Worse than that girl who put her tooth in a glass of sour milk. Ha! I poured the milk in her slippers!" The Tooth Fairy laughed.

She looked under the bed. She checked under the mattress. She peeked in all the boxes on Pearl's table.

She couldn't find Pearl's tooth. So she tore the room apart looking for it.

Morning arrived. Pearl couldn't believe her eyes. Her room was a mess!

Boxes were spilled. Socks were all over the floor. Homework was tossed everywhere.

There was a scribbled note on Pearl's table.

Pearl tried to make out the last words.

"She'll never be able to—to what?"

9. Grounded

Pearl ran her finger over the last words. They were smeared. Water spots that looked like teardrops dotted the page.

"Poor Tooth Fairy." Pearl put her hand to her heart.

"This must be why she needs my tooth so badly. If only I could read it." Pearl squinted at the words.

Opal ran into Pearl's room. "Hey, do you have my—"

She stopped. "What happened here?"

"Nothing." Pearl tucked the letter under her pillow.

Opal backed out of the room. "You're in big trouble," she said.

Dad poked his head in. "What's going on in here? JOAN!" he yelled.

Mom rushed in. She was in her bathrobe.

"Yikes! It looks like a storm hit. What happened?" Mom asked.

Pearl shrugged. "I guess the Tooth Fairy is mad at me."

Dad folded his arms. "A little fairy did this?"

Pearl nodded.

Mom started picking up socks. "I've never seen such a mess."

Dad growled. "Young lady, you're grounded!"

He stomped off. Mom was right behind him.

Pearl closed her eyes. *Why didn't I listen to Lanie and Mom and trade for the wand?*

Pearl picked up her Ping-Pong balls. She picked up her bottle caps.

Mom and Dad came back. They sat on the bed.

Dad puffed up his cheeks. "I don't know what's going on. But it better stop."

Pearl cried, "But the Tooth Fairy—"

Mom held up her hand. "Pearl, honey. The Tooth Fairy isn't . . . she isn't—"

"Real," said Dad.

Pearl showed them the letter. "Then who wrote this?" she asked.

Pearl pointed to the Tooth Fairy's scribbles. "Can you read what this says?"

Mom and Dad squinted.

"I would know what it says if *I* wrote it. Right?"

Mom rubbed her brow.

Pearl paced back and forth. "I'm going to get to the bottom of this."

"Not until you get to the bottom of this mess," said Mom.

Pearl started cleaning her room.

Opal popped her head in. "Good try—blaming your mess on a fairy."

Opal laughed like a donkey. "I'm telling my teacher a troll ate my homework."

Pearl threw a dirty sock at Opal.

That fairy sure made a mess of things.

Her room was a disaster.

She was grounded.

And the worst part was her parents didn't believe her.

She needed proof the Tooth Fairy was real. There was only one thing left to do.

Trap that fairy!

10. The Trap

Pearl tried to skip her soccer game. She told her dad she was sick. Dad said she was fibbing. He made her play.

Pearl couldn't focus on the game. Balls kept whizzing past her head. *Oh, no! Another goal!* thought Pearl.

"Trap the ball!" shouted Coach.

Pearl caught the next ball. "Gotcha!"

The whistle blew. The game was over. Her team had lost 3–0.

Dad told Coach that Pearl couldn't go to the

team's pizza party.

She was grounded.

All because her parents didn't believe her.

Dad drove Pearl home. She went straight to her room.

Pearl thought about the game. The goal net gave her an idea.

Pearl drew up plans.

She'd trap the fairy! Like a soccer ball in a net!

Pearl's mom said goodnight. Then Pearl went to work.

She pulled a wad from her string collection.

She tied pieces together to make a long rope.

She tied the rope to a fishing net. Then she hung the net.

Pearl put her butterfly net beside her bed.

She wanted to have a backup trap.

"Now for some bait," said Pearl.

She couldn't put her own tooth under her pillow. That was too risky.

Pearl searched in her Halloween box.

She found some lips with fake teeth. She broke off a tooth. Then she put it under her pillow.

Now she just had to stay awake.

Pearl did a 100-piece puzzle. No Tooth Fairy.

She played cards. Still no Tooth Fairy.

Maybe she's afraid of the light.

Pearl shut off her bedside lamp. Still no
Tooth Fairy.

Pearl's eyes were about to
close when . . .

CRASH!

"Ow!" came a high
voice in the dark.

Pearl dropped to the floor.

She held her breath.

She heard footsteps come over to her bed.

Swoosh! Down came the net.

11. Face to Face

Pearl turned on the light. The trap worked!

Me oh my. She was not like the fairies in storybooks.

This fairy's wings were floppy. Her hair was frizzy. Her shoes were on the wrong feet.

Pearl felt sorry for her. Then she remembered that this scruffy little fairy had messed up her room. And Pearl was in trouble for it.

The Tooth Fairy threw down the fake tooth. "Let me go, you trickster!" she shouted.

"Say you're sorry," said Pearl.

"For what?" asked the Tooth Fairy. "For waking you up? I've been up all night."

The Tooth Fairy tugged at the net.

"No. For messing up my room," said Pearl.

"Oh, that," said the fairy. "You didn't give me any choice."

"But you broke my stuff," said Pearl.

"I'm sorry. Okay, kid?" The Tooth Fairy sighed.

She waved her magic wand to fix Pearl's room. Sparks shot out every which way.

Then *fffut*. The wand fizzled.

The Tooth Fairy shrugged. "It's broken."

Pearl crossed her arms. So *that's* why she wanted to trade her wand. It was broken.

"I'll get you another one," said the Tooth Fairy. "I promise. Now let me go!"

The Tooth Fairy flew against the net. She bounced off.

"I'm not letting you go until you tell me why you need my tooth," said Pearl.

"Give me the tooth first." The Tooth Fairy reached her hand through the net.

Pearl put her teeth box between her knees. She opened the box.

"This is the first tooth I ever lost," said Pearl.

"You'll grow another one," said the Tooth Fairy. "Now gimme."

"But you have billions of teeth. Can't I have this one?"

"No!" cried the Tooth Fairy. "You can keep your next tooth that falls out. Not this one."

"I won't have a full set of teeth for my collection if you take this," said Pearl.

The Tooth Fairy untied her pouch.

She dumped teeth out on the bed. "Here. Take these. I don't need them."

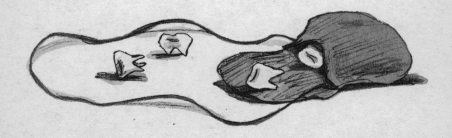

Pearl asked, "But don't you need them to build your castle?"

"It already has five hundred rooms," said the Tooth Fairy.

Pearl started to reach for the teeth. Then she stopped.

"Wait!" she said. "What's so special about *my* tooth?"

Pearl held up the Tooth Fairy's last letter. She pointed to the words she couldn't read.

"What does this say? What won't you be able to do if I don't give you my tooth?"

12. Fairy Dust

The Tooth Fairy tried to squeeze out from under the fishing net.

Pearl grabbed her butterfly net.

"You can't get out," said Pearl. "Not even your wand can help you out of this."

"Okay, okay," said the Tooth Fairy. "I'll tell you why I need your tooth."

She wrung her hands. "I need your tooth to fly again!" she yelled.

"Your wings are for flying," said Pearl.

The Tooth Fairy slapped her head. "My

wings are for steering. Fairy dust makes
me fly."

"Well, I don't have any fairy dust," said Pearl.

"Yes, you do. It's in your tooth."

Pearl picked up her tooth. She shook it.

"It's not *inside* your tooth," said the Tooth
Fairy. "I make dust *from* your tooth."

Pearl turned her tooth
in her fingers. "Why
don't you use a tooth
you already have?"

"A child's first lost
tooth is special," said
the Tooth Fairy. "It's
the only one with the
power."

The Tooth Fairy slumped over. "I'm running out of fairy dust. I need to make more. Or else I won't make it home tonight."

Pearl couldn't believe that her tooth had so much power.

But something sounded fishy.

"Why is mine the only first tooth in the world?" asked Pearl.

The Tooth Fairy rubbed her eyes. "Only second, third, and fourth teeth are falling out."

"Show me how the fairy dust works," said Pearl.

The Tooth Fairy looked in her tiny box. "I only have a pinch of dust left."

"Fly around my room once," begged Pearl. "I'll give you my tooth."

"Promise?" asked the Tooth Fairy.

"Triple promise," said Pearl.

Pearl let the Tooth Fairy out of the net.

The Tooth Fairy reached inside her box. She pinched the last bit of dust. She sprinkled it all over herself.

"Here I go!" she cried.

The Tooth Fairy's wings glowed. She rose and flew like a rocket! A spray of sparkles trailed behind her.

Pearl clapped with glee.

The fairy landed softly on the bed. "A deal's a deal," she said.

Pearl handed over her tooth.

The Tooth Fairy put the tooth in her box. She closed the lid.

A poof of light flashed.

The Tooth Fairy opened the lid. The box was full of fairy dust.

"Thank you, Pearl," she said.

Pearl yawned. The Tooth Fairy pulled back the covers. Pearl crawled under them.

The last thing Pearl remembered was a shower of sparkles.

13. A Tooth for a Tooth

Pearl felt as if she had been asleep for a hundred years.

She rubbed her eyes. She sat up. Her room was all put back together!

Now maybe she wouldn't be grounded any more.

The Tooth Fairy was finally gone. And Pearl's special, magical tooth was gone forever.

Pearl sighed. She missed her tooth.

But she knew it was better as fairy dust than tucked away in a box in her room.

Pearl perked up. "Box? Yes! I still have a

pretty box for another collection!"

A glitter letter leaned against her gold box.

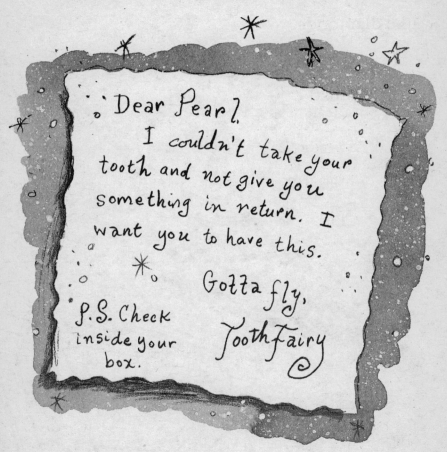

Dear Pearl,
    I couldn't take your tooth and not give you something in return. I want you to have this.

            Gotta fly,
            Tooth Fairy

P.S. Check inside your box.

Pearl opened the lid. A tiny glass bottle lay on the blue velvet.

She held it to the sunlight. Powder twinkled like diamonds.

Pearl gasped.

Fairy dust!